Cressida Cowell * Ed Eaves

Daddy on the Moon

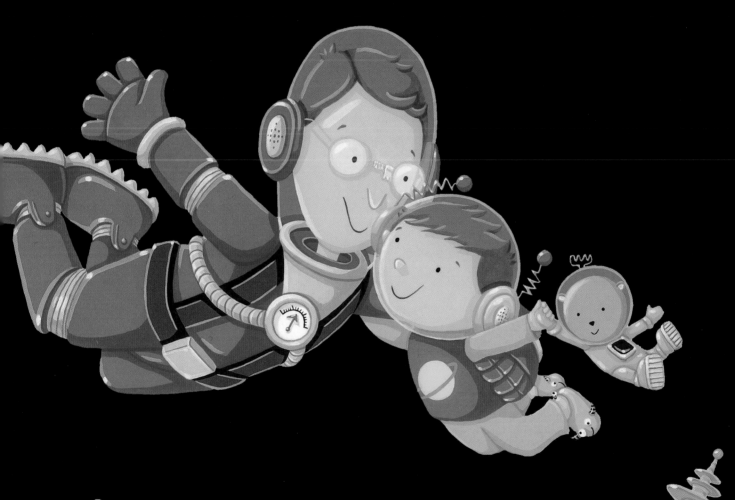

MACMILLAN CHILDREN'S BOOKS

It was bedtime . . .

and Sam was unhappy.

Sam was
unhappy on
the stairs.

Sam was
unhappy in
the bath.

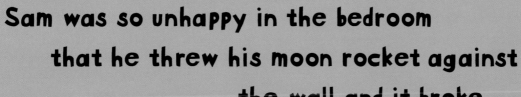

Sam was so unhappy in the bedroom
that he threw his moon rocket against
the wall and it broke.

It broke in two and now Sam
was really unhappy.

Sam's mummy said, "I can mend it, darling.
I AM a qualified mechanic."
But Sam said, "I want DADDY to mend it!"

Daddy couldn't mend it, because Daddy wasn't
here right now. Daddy was working far away.

But tonight he was flying through the night and the dark and the stars to be back home tomorrow morning.

Daddy would be here tomorrow morning . . .

Daddy would be here
tomorrow morning . . .

Daddy would be here
tomorrow morning . . .

But he wasn't here . . .

At that moment something tapped
at the window. It was a . . .

BIG FRIENDLY DIGGER!

"I want my daddy now," said Sam.
"Okay," said the digger. "Just hop
in my scoop and we'll find your daddy."

So Sam hopped into the digger's scoop and Sam and the digger rolled away through the night looking for Sam's daddy.

"What does your daddy look like?" asked the digger. "He's six foot four and he's good at EVERYTHING," said Sam.

Sam and the digger rolled for miles and miles,
but they couldn't find Sam's daddy ANYWHERE.
Suddenly, down sped a . . .

RESCUE HELICOPTER!

"I want my daddy NOW, please,"
said Sam to the rescue helicopter.

"Okay," said the rescue helicopter.
"Climb aboard, but don't touch anything."

"Mayday, mayday! Red alert!
We have lost Sam's daddy.
Seven foot two and eyes of blue."

So Sam and the rescue helicopter
sped through the night, but they couldn't find
Sam's daddy however fast they went.
Suddenly, up whooshed a . . .

SPACESHIP on the way to the moon.

"I want my daddy NOW, please," said Sam to the spaceship.

"Okay," said the spaceship. "Grab a helmet and fasten your seatbelts. We are about to find your daddy

IN SPACE!"

So Sam and the spaceship blasted their way through the earth's atmosphere and sped through millions of miles of inky blackness until they landed . . .

on

the

MOON!

And there, sitting on a rock
having a sandwich, was . . .

SAM'S DADDY!

He had just been mending the Space Station on the moon, and all the aliens were very grateful.

"More sugar, Mr Ponting?" said one of the aliens.
"Oh, Mr Ponting, you're a mechanical genius,"
said the other aliens, all together.

Sam's daddy was SO PLEASED to see Sam.

They waved goodbye to the spaceship because
Sam's daddy said he would take Sam home
in his very own Sooper-Dooper, Sonic-Engined,
Big Blaster Moon Rocket.

And Sam's daddy let Sam drive
ALL THE WAY HOME.

AND WHEN SAM
CAME DOWNSTAIRS
THE NEXT MORNING . . .

To my father, with happy memories
of the Moon Game — C.C.

For Dad — E.E.

First published 2005 by Macmillan Children's Books
This edition published 2005 by Macmillan Children's Books
a division of Macmillan Publishers Limited
20 New Wharf Road, London N1 9RR
Basingstoke and Oxford
Associated companies throughout the world
www.panmacmillan.com

ISBN: 978-0-333-99761-1

Text copyright © Cressida Cowell 2005
Illustrations copyright © Edward Eaves 2005
Moral rights asserted.

5 7 9 8 6

A CIP catalogue record for this book
is available from the British Library.

Printed in China